PRELUDE TO TRANSGRESSION

# PRELUDE TO TRANSGRESSION

M KITCHELL

INSIDE THE CASTLE, 2020

"ONE REACHES THE STATES OF ECSTASY OR OF RAPTURE ONLY BY DRAMATIZING EXISTENCE IN GENERAL."

*Inner Experience*
(Georges Bataille, 1943)

to stare at the sun
& to highlight the distance
is to echo god
in continual distress
*alas, alas, it is night*

—

after the stonescape
the ruining of bodies
the sky alights red
for community falters
& there is now no escape


—

asleep inside the
impossible monument
awakening slow
to a new idea of space
all lost alone inside air

—

height's vicissitude
black sky endowment, absence
& *now man will shout*
penetrating like the hole
to whisper what he now wants

—

there is a secret
that the man's body holds tight
monosyllabic
memory of the glass door
opening to a new sight


——

the shape of the house
zoned forgivability
no insistent space
the mollusk vibrates through lead:
the film exposes nothing

—

seal off the white door
the prayer-like light of sky
the stone in the room
dust on ice, nightmare of white
blind men running in circles

——

the blood spill pours off
the table of the lamb, christ
side-wound split like salve
satiation, hydration
as if the mark on the page

—

the stone of lapis
& the crying of the rock
as a sign of life
words mean exactly nothing
glowing ember of a life


——

echo of a ghost
the scream is not one of pain
impossible night
fingers buried in his hole
laugh in the flesh of bodies


—

holy nudity
an echo of an ennui
spread like legs & ass
nothing blank can ever pass
the red mass, call of the sea

—

sweat of resistance
*i'm the secret in the walls*
i see your body
& the movements it resists:
*collapse into the other*

—

sweat lodge exercise:
accrued energy, last waste
the body is sore:
*he is lost among the fields*
(the space blanks to static here)

PRELUDE TO TRANSGRESSION

FURTHER BENEATH

THE EARTH

“I GONE EXPLORATION OF THE VOID
  GROPING AGAINST THE DAY”

*Survival*
(Danielle Collobert, 1978)

*(the night done, falling)*

. . . overwhelmed by the opening image of *Madame Edwarda*, the drunk man, alone, night, walking pantsless & hard through the street, laughing, holding his sex . . . the idea of the image transported to a here & now: the suited man, alone, taut, hard . . . numb, coasting an overpowering freedom . . .

*(continuity: Élisabeth Blanchard, the great Sufi al-Hallaj, Madame Edwarda)*

> :: to disrupt the narrative of fiction, replace it with
> *rupture* at a moment of climax, reflexion of
> author into the word—the night done,
> falling

28

the idea of constructing sexual desire into
an explorable narrative can only result
in a dissatisfaction                    reality



                                    all art of money
                                    with nothing but
                                          time

the sight of the moon on the horizon
we ball up in the shells of this house
this roomless house

our bodies touch & heat
     follows
& these walls of rock are
     warmed

     ~~but inside this house is a secret / the lower chambers,~~
     ~~cooled by the earth, hold the bodies of those who have~~
     ~~visited the house in a state of refusal / the lower corridors~~
     ~~are filled with the roaming moans of ghosts.~~

     ~~one can't help but be terrified of them on occasion. the~~
     ~~sounds are unfamiliar.~~

we satiate like liquor
our bodies enjoined
a rest passing from the outside

30

~~house / / / next to nothing / / / the bee dies / facing me / / entombed on the white / of a wooden railing / / / house / / / next to death / no / / / the whispers grow louder / for the decision has been / made — that of the / ghosts / / / "we will speak" / / a voice says / / / "we will tell you of / the house " / / / " the house calls death / and this / is home " / / / the house comes to life~~

pool black
white room                    floor
⟡⟡⟡⟡⟡⟡⟡⟡⟡⟡⟡⟡⟡⟡⟡⟡⟡⟡⟡
an air of                     confusion


the left hand
channels   the
dark

            the omens
            carry seed
            of new lies

the right hand      opens the door
                    to the hallway

                    turns the light
                    on

# INSIDE THE BOOK

# I SAW THE EARTH

# INSIDE THE EARTH EARTH

# I SAW THE BOOK

a symphony of hirsute men, nude
        in the desert:                screaming into the sun
                                        one by one


vampiric ontology, a float de-censorial

    *HE'S AN AESTHETE WITH A TASTE FOR BLOOD,*
    *& SHE'S JUST STARTED HER PERIOD*


I decorate the room with bird semen
& let sun burn my forehead to touch the extension—
I carry the question of albino dog shit

    feed on oysters,
    cold ice,
    horseradish & cocktail sauce,

    we shit down with a white

melancholic elasticity of a loneliness, suffering

words misread, misunderstood

~~satellite television~~
~~i'm in love but so busy~~
~~weight of travel~~
~~need for coffee~~
~~insouciant headspace~~

~~fuck box, screams~~
~~too much~~
~~no escape~~
~~so tired~~
~~eventual demise~~
~~humanity is fucking oblivious~~

~~there is no gold in the room~~
~~escape route blocked by seals~~

I guess there is the question of what happens
to art when it's swallowed by narrative
& even then, what can be said of a
narrative of refusal

~~the hiss tape opens up / & the sound near the background~~
~~grabs / my inattention / & shapes my devouring cone /~~
~~twisted to pain / like crunch / the echo of the voice of~~
~~/ the dead~~

~~I am alone saying this / the tape played again / sound~~
~~pushed closer~~

*I am listening*

~~the void calling back like / I found it, the bottom of / the~~
~~wall / like remnant of burn, black / you no recollection~~
~~/ source abandoned / maybe a former inhabitant~~

~~I am listening / all existence / is burning~~

~~like hanging on to existence / I will rewrite what you've~~
~~told me / the space of the question / presented in tape~~
~~hiss~~

~~to listen carefully~~

~~howls, domed enclosure / remembered absence~~

~~the secret is the body memory / of hyperbolic fascism~~

the ruined city
sits                    beyond the horizon

between us & the ruins
lies a forest

past the ruined city / lies the ocean

the sea breeze carries through the
air                    & penetrates our                    thoughts
&                      we find ourselves                   desperate
to discover            the feel of the water               on our skin

[          *perhaps in the ruined city*
           *we can find something*
           *we are looking for*                    ]

transparent materiality
objects buried beneath
dirt, cement, dust

"          we must tear up the grass
           so it will stay green                    "

& we depart with an image

the ruined city, founded upon
the site of the two children's
death                    (a memorial)

to live in a warehouse
windows of glass brick
spiral staircase

like the rest light brings
the subjects into focus

as if the dream state
could ever echo into reality

i'm learning how to answer the
questions           the wrong way

spacing communication into
anamnesis—

the real is still attainable,
it must be made visible

the vertical of the high reach
fulfills like absence never could

the ruined city
sits like romantic fantasy
ignores the suffering inhabitants

    *the immaculate nature of a perfect hairy ass*
    *the holiness of suffering*
    *finds release in a handful of flesh*


to knead like bread                with words that don't rhyme
                              the sun sets on the ruined city
entranced by sea breeze,
the young virgin looks for a man to find solace in

    [        a rending, gashed blood, the
              night howls. the disposability
              of the man is what makes
              him so attractive            ]


the prick guided into the locked wound
the man's insignificance renders violence
a building crumbles as if to echo impotence

how to manage the aesthetic import
of images into words—
    *the sun, I think*

in the story the subject disappears
removed pronoun floating away from
signification

as if movement, dependent on character

no body signaling, only
movement as such, the
head rush of excess upon
confrontation with the
given space of an
event.

cold wind blasts
& fans the flames

behind the house dead pampas grass grows in wait. sighting the flame,
the burn through neutral, imagined scent, speculative, "*forget about it,
he's been dead.*" the voice floating minus solid referent, like an echo or
a ghost, these houses on hills are all doomed as if—

—not    burn,    no
flame, just blood, death, murder spilled sign forgotten narrative—*no
fire only the kill.*

(toolshed as absence, consideration)

*:: the house unfinished*

orphan child murders his adoptive parents in a bout of
/ psychotic / rage / leaving / the house / empty &
available / to a / market / marked / by / desperation
/ & sadness / too / much / to go / around around / &
the exception being / though / of another location / a
/ solution / given to / the desire of /     location

*:: basement drywall*

burnt skin—the flames never too far away—

*:: the question in the room*

but the muddled dialog is drowned out by the
peaking levels of the music on the soundtrack
the degraded film-stock, entropy licensed out

nothing sensible of whatever the thought—bodies in the field—
vegetables choked as an afterthought—dead leaves blood spill

FOREST

WOUND

"BORN FROM A HOLE. BUILT AROUND A HOLE. I
AM AN ORGANIZATION OF THE EMPTINESS."

*Extracts from my body*
(Bernard Noël, 1972)

It is under mysterious circumstances that he loses his way in the forest. He thinks he is looking into a mirror but he is only gazing at a reflecting pool. The wind pushes through the trees, inducing a violent, static hum. In discovering that he is lost, the man encounters a specific effusion that ties his fear to a fresh desire. Sweat drips from his brow upon his shirt, diffusing materiality to reveal the shapes of hidden flesh. Light flickering between branches begins to resemble fog in its capacity to disorient. There is no doubt that the man is lost.

He begins to panic. Before him are the trunks of two felled trees and he hears the sound of screaming. He feels himself entombed in the open space, cemented into a posture of desperation. He knows that he must move forward. The spectral glow of the forest is enticing—an overlapping of day and night in perpetuity. Fading from distraction to quietude, any discovery is suspicious. He must move forward.

He walks through the trees alone and lost. He glows with desire and fear, a relentless sweat marking lust and physicality. A sensation of a *task* encroaches upon him, a necessary direction. The forest presents a space for communication with the dead.

The forest offers labyrinthine corridors to wander, but the design of a maze imposes a single correct route to any *dérive*. Otherwise, a drunken space. In desire and fear the man welcomes an intoxicated effusion. The speech of the earth sounds behind him, as if it were the ground screaming in pain. The air calls for removal or collapse. A vertiginous quickening finds the man vibrating in the dirt.

An unknowable sensation.

survival without
       continuity


                                                            vibratory speech


the gestures of the body
the air in its hold
there is no past


gestures                                    (sacrificial words)
                                                      (worlds)


               ecstatic
               suffering
               predicated by
               earlier loss


        and        there        can        not        be        a        totality


(imageless desuetude)


                              "MOVE FORWARD"
                                                →


(all the dead appear
  in a beam of light)

                                        continuity without
                                        understanding


auto-
annihilative autonomy
as if the sun
could break through
branches



penetrate
this shake




                         (intoxication)
                         (insensate
                                 wh ● le)



        the        shape        of        the        body        alone




    the shake inhabits the scream — the day strikes the body
    and I can feel the glint of heat, sweat — no — there is
    nothing but desire to touch — this placed dejection
    — sweatlodge anxiety complicated by erasure of


                                                    the presence

## 2

The lost man opens his eyes to find the day sliding into night. The light coming through the trees gradually dims. The man becomes afraid. His body is strong but alone he has no one to confront. A duplicitous refusal. He stands up and begins to walk.

The labyrinthine monotony of the forest mutes anxiety and finds the man ensconced in the fading light. He begins to disassociate from his surroundings. Colors dim to neutral. Inside of the flatness his feet no longer meet the ground. In considering the reality of his situation he can do nothing but close his eyes. In this aphonic void, his body jolts into a solid, unseen object. He has run into a tree.

Opening his eyes the tree towers before him. His gaze casts from the base up, an inescapable tellurian verticality. His own stature is dwarfed in comparison. The man begins to small.

Submission creates a constraint that becomes appealing. Removing his clothes, his body meets the ground. His hands explore the body with which he no longer feels a rapport. The feeling of his hand, caressing his skin, inhabits a pleasant numbness. He watches his sex rise to the air, the tingling disconnect between head and flesh positioning an acute sensation of depersonalization. He starts to laugh.

From the ground he sights the tops of trees above him. He can no longer hear the world. Night has almost overwhelmed the day, and in darkness he will recede into landscape. He will sink into the chthonic pulse of a world he is no longer apart from. The sustain is prolonged beyond expectation. In numbness the night welcomes him. He is neither cold nor warm, but absent.

The eroticism of the body he now finds himself outside of exists only in vague remembrance, the uncanny sensation tied to a corporeality distanced from the mist he evaporates into. Night has come.

the dark is doubled
tactile memory


        the search for a body


                ( & the voice whispers:
                  *so give me a body*" )


        eroticism & death
        stand together, as
        unknowable, impossible

        (unknowable other than
          through an
                other)


torn, come-stained shirt
exegetic flesh
insides pushing out
absorption


                the night

before — if I,
to touch — the
body I inhabit, not
escapable, possible,
line the voices of
the trees, violating,
unapproachable,
negation as sexual
f u l f i l l m e n t ,
listening to the
dead speak, with
the spectrality, the
sound of the forest's
night, distanced
from the world,
interchange, the
body the ground,
absolution, finality,
approbation into
scent.

night, inescapable

the search for a body


follow the route like a path
into a ruinous abyss



the man in the earth


this telluric image

                                        there can be
                                        no self


                                        only resistance



                only night
                        only

                        & in the black
                        night—
        there is         nothing,

                        no light.

3

The man has been lifted from the forest floor. He is being carried through the forest, unconscious. [It seems, at this point, that the narrator has encountered an absence.] In the cosmic hierarchy, this is not important.

His body is placed onto a stone slate. A fire is lit. The night is black.

*We are all accomplices of betrayal.*

*We find the man's body and pick it up, many of us. We carry him through the forest to the clearing we have already prepared. We strip ourselves of clothes and in this gesture we unite in ritual.*

*We set the body upon a table of stone. Our bodies move, positioned into a circle, each of us equidistant from the man. Turning, we circle the stone table in procession. With the momentum of our circulating bodies, an energy is established. Our voices unite in hymn. The tonalities we can express, discordant but united, establish the mood required.*

*Stilling our circumambulation, our gaze returns to the new body. We reach our arms, our hands, to the mouth of he who is next to us. We cover the mouth and our song is muted. It becomes violently determined in its reticence. It pales to a muddled atonality.*

*Next, our hands reach to another's eyes. In blindness the reality of our event inhabits what it is we are after. There is no unity in our desire, only the vitality of cohesion. The man's body begins to glow in the darkness of the night.*

*We remove our hands. Our bodies still in posture to a gesture of solitude, of finitude. Even we cannot understand our presence.*

*We want to speak to the man but know that in his inaction he can make no response. We want to apologize for what will take place momentarily, but the reality is we feel no guilt.*

One by one we break our static nature and carry stones that surround our clearing. The stones are heavy but our solid bodies, accustomed to the transport of felled trees and debris have readied us for this difficulty.

With the stones, we approach the man. In our silence, we all understand his beauty, the desirous nature of his being, the arousal of lust. Individually, we can each appreciate our own sex. We pay no attention to the sex of any other at this point. We are in the solitude of communication: our bodies with that of the man.

With grunts of effusion we strike the man's body. We lose track of the night and the nature of temporality. We lose control. Soon we are covered with blood and our desperate lust is transferred to we who surround one another.

The abeyance of the man is no longer of our concern. The glow has dulled but still illumines shape, enough to reveal our bodies. The desire we feel is overwhelming. There is nothing we can imagine taking place anywhere than the space we inhabit now.

We paw at one another with thick and hirsute arms. Soon our flesh is mounded with the others. There can be no end in sight, for all of time is as impossible as death. We spend hours indulging in the pleasure flesh offers, suppurating an appeal to the gods of the night.

One by one our seed spills: whether onto the ground, into or upon one another. We are lost entirely to exhaustion and effusion. There is nothing to say.

caked mud dries to death mask
he takes it off the face
& places it over his own




a movement of transition,
aggravated momentum




to even approach desire

4

The man is probably dead.
The man is probably dead.

His body prostrate in the forest clearing, nude and beautiful, still. When a finality is suggested it must be questioned. This is a statement of fact based on the idea that the world keeps turning. One day, it will not. It is at this time that finitude will encounter no resistance.

If all the trees in the forest were to fall there would not be a crash loud enough to wake the sleep of the dead. There is always the question of whether or not the dead can dream. Only the thrilling agony of collapse. In death resemblance returns to no image, no silence, only to oneself or god.

Embedded in annihilation, the initiate wants to speak to god, so god speaks from a stone:

> IF THERE IS A FORM IN SERVICE TO A REVOLUTION IT IS NOT ORATION. IN DIALOG THERE MUST BE TWO INDIVIDUALS AVAILABLE TO SPEAK. THERE IS NOTHING TO SAY ALONE OTHER THAN STATEMENTS IN PRAISE OF SILENCE. THERE CAN BE ONLY TRAGEDY, EROTICISM, AND COMEDY. ALL MEN SPEAK WITH THEIR FOOT IN THEIR MOUTH. AFFIRMATION CAN BE DESCRIBED AS A HECATOMB OF WORDS SANS GOD OR REASON, WHICH IS TO SAY IN ABSENCE. DEFINITION OF HECATOMB: ANY GREAT SLAUGHTER. ONE CANNOT CREATE THE SACRED WITHOUT PARTICIPATION IN SACRIFICE.

God speaks as if existence is a gamble, and within this thought the man recovers from his death.

again — with eyes
open — I walk —
through the forest
— I touch the rock —
and the rock touches
back — a new nudity,
birthed with dawn —
remembrance — or
if only an echo of a
once-held    linearity
—    dispersion,    all
through the air — new
holes where the body
can   be   pummeled
— like god's speech,
inherently   dejected
— touch, or scream,
only a ledge to put the
body upon

labyrinth as preposition

more residue                                        (come
                                                    sweat
                                                    blood
                                                    shit)

it is my body that
must be forced
into the day



sensual insistence



memory abandoned
new birth



day is coming

the clouds push          away

from the earth

The man sits up. He realizes that if he were to cut his own flesh he would push syntax to the state of disintegration, but he has no sharp object at his disposal.

[One must take a moment to consider the syntactical organization of the maze, especially when considered in the dark. Paths that lead to nowhere, winding intoxication. The space refuses to settle into utility, offering only the folly of disorientation.]

The man, dirtied from his fall, licks the dust off of his wounds. (A confrontation between the man and his oblivion.)

In the stream near the pool in which he has cleansed his body, the man finds the figurehead of a horizontality—the common earthworm. Mutated in nourishment of the forest, the worm strikes the man as large, abject, frightening. But for the man, post-death, any metonym of physicality can serve only the sensual culmination of rapture.

Finding his own body once again present, the man, now clean, rises like the sun and begins to walk. In recalling the ancestral nature of this place, the forest of his disillusionment, the man realizes what it is he is looking for. In echo of the body, the wound, the gash, the hole: the variable insistence found in breath, sound, sight, excrement, urine, scent, totality.

[…]

A decrease in the potentiality of voice: the light has come. The man addresses the void the cavern presents and walks forward into the day.

2ND PRECEDENT TO

THE DISAPPEARANCE

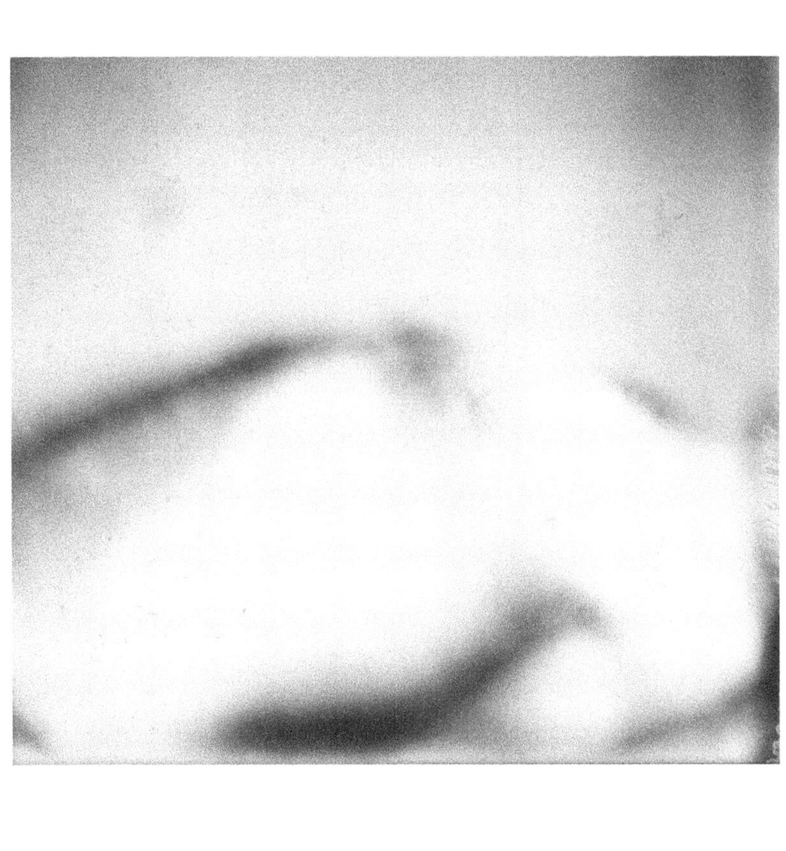

“I'M IN LOVE WITH A NIGHTMARE,
AND AM THE INCARNATION OF INFERNAL GAIETY.”

*Clodia—Fragmenta*
(Franco Brocani, 1981)

[    ECHO      LIKE
SOUND     SAYS            ]
RADIO  STATIC

↓

IF
        there were more than three voices to be heard
which of these voices would be the one that echoes

which would haunt

which would cry
which would          scream

        *there are so many of them, all of these voices*
        all functioning in light

                        ↓

        the site echoes & speaks
        sound falls into the dark
        peals of laughter          & sweat

$\downarrow$

*we talk to each other like there is no one there*
*say hello to me next time you pass*
*think about all the photographs in the world*
*what utility could these images serve*
*there's nothing in the world that's a secret*

$\downarrow$

talk to me through the night

$\downarrow$

the act of writing is one of colonizing the empty page
we can't control everything       *not even silence*
there is nowhere that understands the shape of the sky
coming over the horizon

$\downarrow$

*i'm talking to you in my sleep,*
*these are messages*

↓

the dark penetrates the site and speaks to the air
the air laughs back, like always
images of genitalia reverberate in retinal zones

*i'm calling the echo and expecting a response*

↓

let's walk, let's walk around this idea
    the pretense is never expected, but
    there is no one else around

&
what if this is the answer
            [*no no no no no*]

↓

TELL ME ABOUT THE LIGHT THE LIGHT TELL ME
ABOUT THE LIGHT THE LIGHT TELL ME ABOUT

::

the echo / the silence / the stone

::

↓

stacked feet onto sand pushed down buried bones like dark beneath something always something else there are cracks the sand seeps through fills all holes until there is nothing but positive space the world's detriment ~~crabs crawl through & the child was prevented from kicking the crab & children are born through capital in order to become killers & this is not exclusively a problem it is exclusively human~~ & we can pretend to know anything else— amythest whistle like the shine the shine the shine stuck in this loop can't find the best escape route the hallways keep shifting realigning & dominating force never wants the gesture of return wants nothing but nothing but nothing but echo the present in an infinitely      crowded circle

↓

*(the language you tell in cannot be true)*
*(the language i loan you can only lie)*
*(i'm looking for meaning, it seems to have gone)*

↓

the night came loud that night
in the weight of the night i pushed
the tension generated heat, held long as

*i could.*

↓

this long was not long enough & still the echo followed the night
again & again & again & again & again &


repeated movement of the way language forms meaning
a memory that is       the only escape
the weather lies beneath the silence of
what it was that tunneled from within

↓

if abstraction is a silence the void
can abyss into understanding

to die in the night is a trap

↓

*only the sun can call like the siren*
*everything i write is a letter i want to burn*

.

.

↓

the echo, still

↓

body positioned inside of the cave the sound empty like house static blaring from signal invisible to the touch—inexact nature of a body form new shapes the turn the gesture the way flesh means meat when seen at an angle of desire—the sudden movement presenting an interruption to the shake of earth like walking the lip of a volcano or being enclosed upon by water—the number of videos available in the world of tsunamis crashing upon a shore brinking destruction death & in revealing the finite nature of personhood (as if sound could stand in the way of the object, as if the radio couldn't pulse the interior bones themselves) or form— when the reverberation echoes to formless the body pulsates a blatant eroticism met like the zone of self-penetration by object or—when the reverberation echoes to formless the body pulsates a blatant eroticism met like the ecstatic placation of dizziness, vertiginous fall into the night

↓


A SENSE OF VERTIGINOUS PARODY OF OBSCENITY
& THE SACRED

↓

still, the echo

↓

they walk & discuss the space of the words
& forget about everything else

*what are you trying to get away from?*

*is there a way to escape it?*

*can I become a participle in the text?*


hesitate to let the question mark return, rhetorical questions
perhaps

↓


the echo inside of the dark sounds like it can listen, respond,
react

↓

on the count of three
please return your eyes to the wall

           1   2   3

the wall will ripple its sensual expectations
will sweat the damp air that keeps these plants awake

↓

on the count of three
we talk about the echo


    1      2      3


we face the echo again, the echo asks about the body &
what happened to it
we ask the echo if he means the house
the echo says no, he means the body


one and both are the same, like the book & the life


the echo laughs, but it was us who began to laugh first.

↓

*& we & we & we want to know about the light*
*(tell us about the light)*

the echo looks confused

"why have you doubled the self"

| | |
|---|---|
| we are all ok here | here in the light |
| we are all ok here | here |
| here | in the light |

↓

*the eternal thirst for an impossible death*
*is like the glow of the ember'd orb*
*ejected from flame*

# THE DOUR RECTUM

*as the voice throws itself into the void*

a category of commitment | a stabilization of the image
delicacy, power & violence—"I would like to be a stranger,
or to say the least,

                           estranged."

language is still an opaque void, no blind light at the end
of the film […]

windows canceled by light, birds call like a screaming reticence
    toward the manifestation of a world not stilted by terror
    ONLY TO LAUGH IN THE FACE OF DEATH: this
    world, of course, fits the funds of many others, the misery
    that speeds like light causes still stasis not battery voltage;
    NO WRITING IS GENDERED—the pen is only a pen is
    if your Freudian insistence slights the word itself.


for the words to burn WHITE HOT there must be the reflection
    of the sun upon the sea, an annulled solar anus, the pineal eye
    blinking from the death-rose of the impossible.


    FILL THE POEM WITH FLOWERS
    LET THEM GROW LIKE NARRATIVE
    LIKE THE SEED PLANTED: THE BODY
    IS A GROUND, IS A RECTUM, IS THE

seduction of the throat, this is not a stage it is a space, not a space but a void [fixated on this idea, its contemporary presence] to pause and say something TRYING TO WRITE A TEXT HERE this a rejection of what one could insist must be learned but classicism is dead while classist tendencies stride forward in the light of this excessive sun.

THE SUN JUST SCREAMS EITHER "FUCK" OR "FUCK YOU" AND THE ENERGY IN BOTH FIND EQUIVALENCE

the seat is equidistant from all four walls & without windows the body is safe from the light. the body crawls on the ground. light bulbs attached to cords strewn throughout the room. walls painted white, floor painted white, body painted white. desiring a flatness. a flatness that defeats this endless horizon.

avoiding proper nouns to increase shelf life
quoting not god but the idea of god itself
the idea of a certain destroyed life: the mannequin of existence
gaining nothing by understanding that there are no answers
the sound the sky makes when it refuses subjectivity is that of a
thundering
                             moan, resistant to echo
                             —because of this flat


the idea that body language communicates more than voice
if it were possible to pantomime light, language's futility would
speak
      bodies piling up like words
      the corporeality of this fucking sheet of paper
      cuts finding blood: disembody the voice to a haunt
but maybe it's just looking for an answer in perfect geometry




that hope should be so impossible

## THE BOTTOM OF A PIT OR THE TOP OF A HIGH-RISE

the spectacle of the spectral
                                        icicles crash to ground in sound
like landscape could communicate anything but feeling like the night,
                                        only the night


                the chorus of refusal, the chorus of—no


the chorus of the void in the static scream of the wireless superego
this endless stream of communication, the warm bath of effluvia
the over-spill of screams, *FUCK ME* like this night


                                (onomatopoetic resistance—
                                like "reality" is what sounds)


cultural amnesia because who needs condoms when you have money

                    it—then, transpires—or so to say—
                    complying with—naught feeling—
                    of desire—night tears—refusal—
                    this silence—negation—dirt—the
                    touch of skin—bleeding sun—*try*


airspace found to be set on fire
planes crashing into buildings
the police exist only to be destroyed
hand shoved inside christ-wound | lamb's blood-drip
fried chicken sunsets, prehensile suppositories
*there's a body at the end of the page*
silt & slime, this mucous, subterranean holy ritual
            (without sunlight god would have never been invented)
the mystic heartache a spiral of entropy
cacti molding of too much water ::



                    an understanding of thirst,
                    the thirst for annihilation,
                    everyone all alone in the white room

CURIOUS AS TO HOW IT FEELS
TO BE BURIED ALIVE IN DIRT,
TO DROWN DRY, NO SPACE TO COUGH


the hollow body communicating like a spirit—sun burnt
hand taken as a mark from god—religious ecstasy eyes like
both death & orgasm—sincerity reinterpreted through the
lens of a becoming, swimming at light-rate—memories of
interpretation—is this a silence or a lie—is there sand beneath
the feet—how many sounds can the ocean be said to make.


    the serial repetition of daily life.
    coherency directed by only power & money.
    blind to trajectory.
                outside of silence.

## THE FLOAT OF SILENCE FLIGHTED INTO AIR & SPEED LIKE DEATH

but this is not approaching mystery. a sound like a thud. the vision of no pointed direction. communicative voice. like the preposition directs. insert: tasting sweat. the mist in the air hazes a green. sight's disposition tainted by a womb-like sea. engendered hold. night comes like a teenager. sized crustaceans clambering out of holes. sexuality is always mediated by swamp. murk like early morning vision. insert: nothing buried beneath the sand. mouthing words devoid of sound. touching one hand to another.

privilege like heat death—regrettably committing to futility—there is
always something          that needs to be done          inside    of
the nothingness—shattering window panes with glass bricks—the
necessity of marking a trajectory through space—trees in a forest—
insert: commentary on a simultaneous obsession & terror of sex—
insert: a guide to believing service work is not useless & defeating—
insert: the scream, the cries, of the damned

                vegetation chants death—
                refreshing like carbonated water—
                hide in the corridors of the war bunker—
                count down from ten and cover your eyes,
                the end of the world will come as no surprise.


affected by disappointment, significantly marked
for a future inside of this building
any sign of life would reflect the world like black glass.

what is the name of this sound.


APATHETIC MISOGYNY BROADCASTS
ALL CHANNELS. THE HEAT BURNS.
NO ONE NOTICES, FEWER CARE.
TERROR MIGHT EASILY BECOME
OVERWHELMING. BEHIND THIS, A MARK.

no future to expect these trees to mature into.
the arrogant precipice lingers in all minds.
how San Francisco's Golden Gate Bridge
carries more self-sacrifice than a Christian
Martyrology.     non-speculative     numbers
blurred like pencil marks. an expectation of
impermanence. collide or collapse. the market-
value of these words fails to leave any sort of
impression. hidden beneath the desk & next to
the pile of come, dried, spilled to the blankest
idea of self-satisfaction. bins of rotten produce.


misspelled apology spent like the smoke of bonfire.
empty rounds fired into water. not even a ripple effect.
lyricism seems either naïve or insincere.
this issue of privilege.
nights blending into days.
what malady. what affliction. a resolute sense of *no*-ness.
interstitial headspace taken over by ivy.
rhizomatic obsession over empty space.

(go slowly)




(let pause space the evening)




(memory just gets in the way)

identity should be as permeable as fiction. any
narrative should hold the fantastic. the primeval
nature of creation & destruction rings more
true than language. the sound of a knife cutting
into flesh. the mush of viscera. give away all
your money. nothing could matter any more

sight
the
bird
flying
away
from
the
sky

sex fantasy just rings empty. its the act that
counts. no ice in the bucket. self-manifested
waking nightmares. need something to get away
from.

LIKE A HOLE, A SUCK OF
PRESENCE, THE FISTED
ALTERITY OF THE SELF

people falling from buildings to a doomed span of narcissism—the hold of one word over another—density forgotten—everything spread out—colors presented on the pavement like eyeshadow—don't  shout AMERICA because nobody believes you—tubes in every orifice—watching foliage through windows in a dimmed light—the birds are still calling—the birds are still calling—

        find a way around the house.
        rectilinear void damage.
        (flat tired)

                      sympathy
        with the redundancy


      avant-
      e  x  i  s  t  e  n  c  e


    mere memory
                             (like sunlight)
      eternally ephemeral, is this night or nowhere
          a predicated collapse into mediocrity


        sun burn the mark of a dry god



            CUT

insert: an emotional core.
insert: the path around the house.
insert: the proof of this refusal.
insert: the reflecting skin
insert: ponds filled with a dark bile
insert: an excuse for a lack




RE-TAKE

as the voice throws itself into the void

a category of commitment | a stabilization of the image
delicacy, power & violence—

language-based   reconnaissance.   revolutionary   impulse.
sounds heard when the ear is placed against the wall. non-
verbal communication of colors. lightning fields populated
by the space of zero. overtaking flight with finitude. calling
god like zero. intoxication of an elemental solitude. nudity.
cold.

"I would like to be a stranger, still."

DIM DEAD BOY

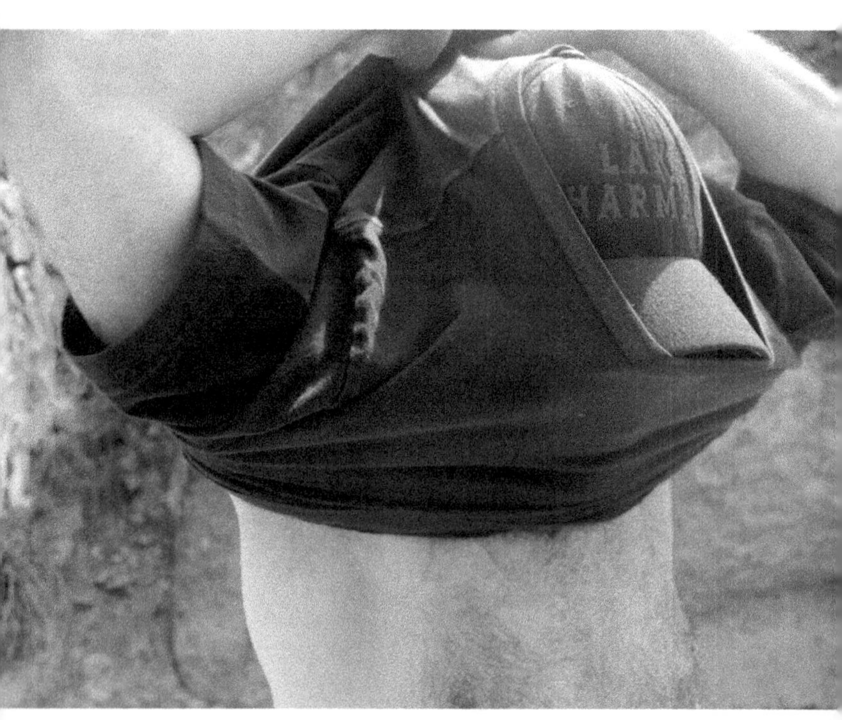
L.A.
HARM

LOVE ME ZADDY

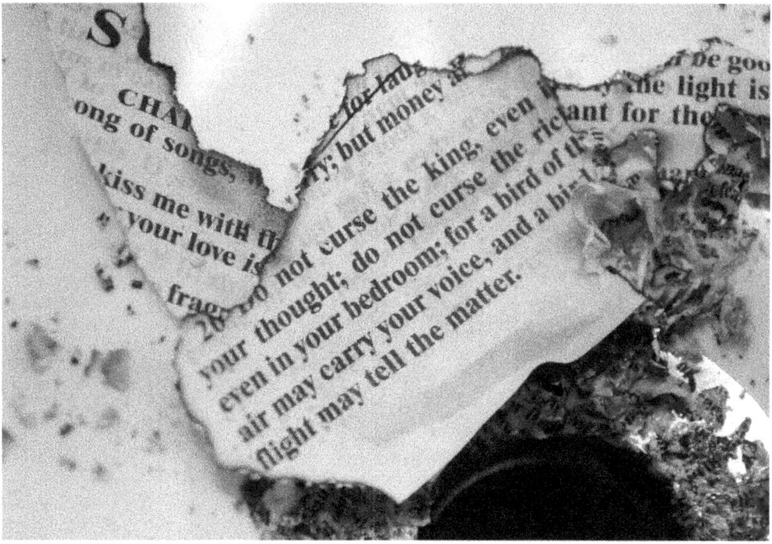

ong of songs,
kiss me with
your love is
y; but money
not curse the king, even
your thought; do not curse the ric
even in your bedroom; for a bird of
air may carry your voice, and a bi
flight may tell the matter.
the light is
ant for th

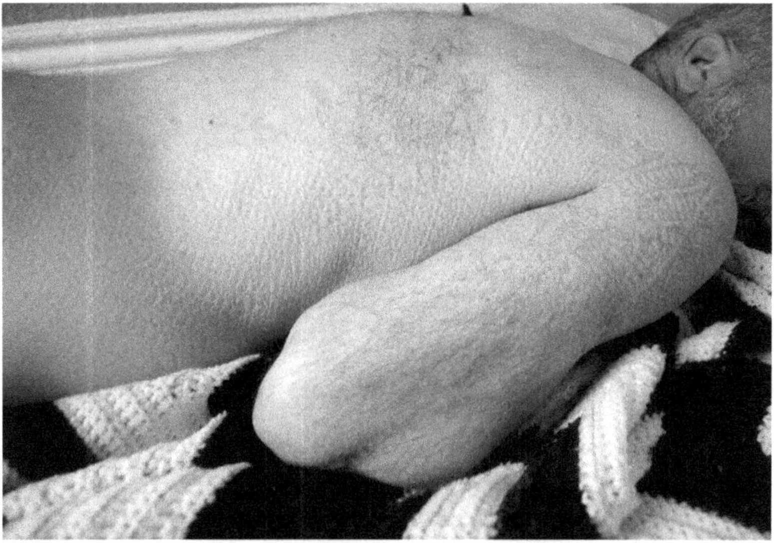

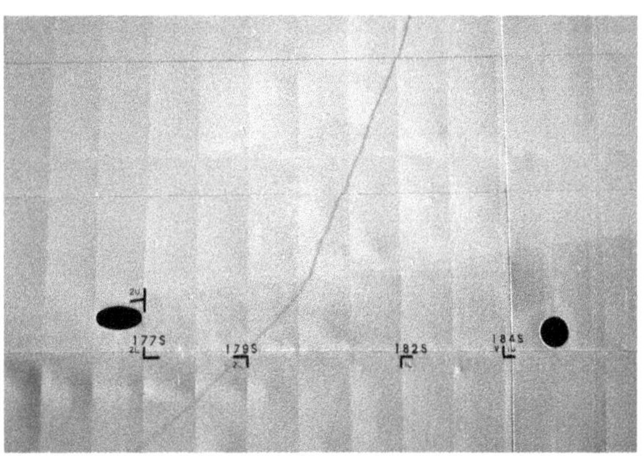
2U
177S
2L
179S
2L
182S
1L
184S
V

ISLAND

"REALITY CLOSES OVER WHAT TOOK PLACE LIKE THE SEA OVER A DROWNING MAN. HE RISES AGAIN ONLY AS A DEAD MAN. BUT THE FORGOTTEN—THE FORGOTTEN IS THE SUBSTANCE OF THE SEA..."

*The book of the forgotten*
(Bernard Noël, 1978)

If the ship were to sink the wreckage of the vessel would constellate into an image indicative of the night. (In this instance all fragmented narrative refuses insistence that *the captain is in control*). An island, being a body of land surrounded by water, can be reached only by boat.

the sea
alone and
motionless black

impenetrable movement
the echo of night

to traverse                    the sea
from terrain
to terrain

          float
impenetrable

the sea
solar black
refusing echo                  reflection
shadows pleated
a voice                        the wind

the world was built invisibly

black                an unapproachable form
the sea              a secret night

1

The sea swims past the boat—a forward movement that erases any misdeed of light—the way reflection is a visible echo—the way echo is an audible reflection—the trip takes several hours, this is the banality of being inside of time and space—the space the man occupies upon the boat is a small room, set apart from the main cabin, hidden, for the crew must not see him—a pause, the man gasps for breath and out the window he can see the foam of waves against darkly hewn wood—for the boat must only transport goods, for the island is home to little but a research facility, the focus, the goals of which the man is not sure, but he knows that she works there, at least part time, and she has asked him to come—the man cannot remember if he'd been asked to come recently, was the letter received yesterday? the week before? the month before? sometimes there are difficult decisions to be made.

space

THE LIGHT
MOVES ACROSS
THE SEA LIKE
THE SHAKE OF
EARTH

AN ERUPTION IS
NOT ALWAYS AN
INTERRUPTION

TIME MOVES
LIKE THE
FLICKER OF
LIGHT

The boat docks under the veil of night. It seems as if day could never come. The man makes his way out of the boat invisibly, as if movement were a gift of absence. He may have drowned & along the beach he finds a shard of glass to examine his reflection. With this, he can continue. The question that haunts the island itself is not whether the man himself is a ghost, for he of course is, but the question configures itself in relation to how he has returned when it was believed he had never left.

*The man's memory lies scattered, and in this moment he cannot remember if it is he who was murdered or if it was he who murdered another.*

The night feels like an enormous room. The air screams like the ticking of a clock. The man cannot accept nature without the mechanical impetus that follows industrialization. The plants all seem fake even though he understands they cannot be. He pushes away the rocks on the shore in the hope of clearing a plate of glass that will operate as a window to the inside of the island. (The noise of the natural is maddening, it is insistent, it refuses rhythm, it escapes repetition in favor of inconclusive echoes—*everything resembles something else*). It is always the unavailable, the unseen that drives desire.

# HE TURNS AWAY
# FROM THE
# LAND TO FACE
# THE FORMLESS
# SEA

atonalwalkawayfromseatothebuildingthebuildingtheinstitute
alongthewayadogcaughtintheroadinthenightthelightreflecting

                                                                                                                                                                        &    it is now he runs through the
forest next to the sea in the
darkness of night


the light of his run, flickering
primordial shadows

as if with the cinematic apparatus,
corneal disturbance – cones & rods
(& light, always light)

2

(through the window: an image of a young girl having bandages
removed from her eyes)


(through the window: the young girl stares ahead of her as if there
could be nothing but the night of god in sight)


(through the window: a new image is imposed upon the young
girl—an image of the night, impossible when considering that the
sun is high above in the clear sky)




(          as if: the sky were not clear in the way the
            clouds let the sun through)




(          as if: inescapable light, distance)

The man cannot find the door so he climbs in through the window. The image of the young girl is gone but there is blood pooling upon the white of a cot.

The room seems primitive in considering what he knows of the institute:

1. the institute is fully funded by government organizations located on 4 of the 7 continents
2. the institute was founded in part to explore the tellurian detritus considered resultant of what a misguided academic once termed parapsychology
3. the institute was founded in part to map the cthonic geography considered generative of psi activity
4. the institute is located on this island for a specific reason, but the reason is unknown
5. the institute is staffed by men and women who, after accepting their position, never return to the world at large
6. the only public results of the institute's research involve video technology and a metonymic exploration of volcanic flow and priapic eruption; how this relates to the aforementioned goals of the institute is unknown

Aside from the cot, there are several items in the room the man finds worthy of note:

1. A thick white rope. The rope could be used to tie a boat to dock, or it could be use to bind the hands and feet of a man. The bondage could be resultant of disagreement, violation, or simple pleasure. In consideration of his own tastes, the man counts all variations as options. In a flash of white light, he realizes that he can hear no sounds in the room.

2. A pair of black boots. The leather on the boots looks worn, as if aged in the sun. The laces are frayed but holding up. The diminutive size of the boots call to mind that of a smaller body, perhaps lean instead of thick. Or perhaps the boots belong upon the feet of the young girl.

3. A bouquet of flowers, left out of water, certainly on their way to death. The man binds the bouquet together in his hands and walks around the room. If someone were to walk into the room at this point—seeing the man dripping with sweat and confusion, holding a bouquet of flowers—a series of questions would follow that the man would have no answers to. He returns the flowers to the table, letting them spread and disperse, falling flat from the cylindrical shape in which his hand gathered them.

Seeing the empty bed, now, the man mistakes the visual implications of the scene for the trauma he would face in encountering an actual murder. The man remembers, from this point forward, not an empty room with a bloodied cot, but rather he remembers an eroticized murder of the young girl whom at one point had her eyes bandaged with white gauze. Any other narrative is empty.

The building is shaped of hallways and by walking these hallways the man forgets the space of the murder he has witnessed. One hallway pulls him away from light and further beneath the earth. It is here that he notices new equipment, electronic monitors, filtered air, and flashing lights. The walls still feel like earth as if to dig one could find the bones of ancestors. Before the institute was granted control of the island it was occupied by Russian fur traders who, after skinning all the native pinnipeds, found themselves trafficking murre eggs.

> *one man recalls nothing but the shape of eggs*
> *& the absent moans of*
> *a thousand skinned seals*
> *—a chorus of misery*

He tells me, "This is when the flies showed up, beckoned by the voiceless echoes carried across the winds."

The shape of the island never seems to have changed, and the only photographic approximations that recall the island with any sort of authority are images distorted by the substantial grain of high-speed film. Digital technology misses the whole for what can be found in the four borders of the image's frame—but in every fleck of grain, one can understand the island's shape.

3

Murre eggs are cauterized in neutral colors that occasionally shift into tonalities on the cooler side of turquoise, mint, & seafoam. They are speckled with distinctive patterns of spots and splotches which determine maternal relationships between the egg and adult birds. In addition, the marks serve as a litmus test for the men and women who collect the eggs: read for image-signification, the eggs could tell the future, the present, or the past. The problem is the fact that, more often than not, time, on the island, was and always will be delineated in such a way that no one can tell if the eggs offer prophecy or reflection.

Because common murre lay their eggs on the rocky sea cliffs of the island, murre eggs are exceptionally pointed. If the eggs were to get jostled, this shape prevents them from rolling over the cliff into the crashing waves of the sea. Despite this, the institute has a collection of 14 murre eggs found at the bottom of the sea, encased in a shell of volcanic effluvia cooled by the water. A fifteenth egg, recently discovered across the island from the initial batch, was scanned using laser technology & opened. Inside of the egg the institute found a grotesque approximation of the common murre, bloated by asphyxiation. It is thought that the heat provided by volcanic flow steadied just long enough, before being cooled by the sea, for the bird (already matured to near the point of hatching) to progress through the remaining stages of development, only to find itself pecking to stone instead of the light of day. If birds had developed speech at some point in their time on this planet, it is sure that this creature would have been heralded as either a martyr or a deity, for such is the nature of sacrifice.

A dish of fried murre eggs and abalone—thinly sliced & beaten raw, rubbed with volcanic sea salt—is often prepared for those who wish to communicate with the dead. Oil left on the plate after the meal is consumed is best used as a salve for open wounds. However, rather than healing, this salve prolongs the wounds' presence upon the body.  While the wound remains it may be probed by the pearl of the abalone, a ritualistic act that results in a suppuration, a pus, which, when dried & made into tea, is said to extend the life by 28 days for every consumed ounce.

4

in forward momentum
the violent insistence to seek
intimacy with absent voices

your body has no space to
touch or ground upon

aphonic figuration of
hands feeling dirt to gesture
without movement there can be
no glide

crescendo of a recollection
a death blow dealt upon the
sounds he would make
as a child

there can be only confusion
in the hallway

projection of thoughts across
rooms and cavernous holes
the ground offers protection
from the phenomena of light
but the light takes the particles
and the emptiness offers
a place for thought to
bury

staring at the sky from the
eyes upon the body upon
the earth the stars show
a map that can only be
retained when abandoned
vocalization enunciates
the memory

placeless island absent island
[aberrant island occulted island]
locatable where but not when

the sky holds the shout of
that landscape
the only body in motion

his finger digging into the
wound and pulling out
the pearl

whispered shouts of endless
suffering as scientific impetus

(video screen flashes movement)
(the display RGB desperate to reintroduce
the earth's natural intensity)

neutral fluorescent
neurological exploration of
color fields

meditation sessions exploiting
the sound of crashing waves

the only death that cannot
be encountered is your own.


After endlessly wandering the halls of the now seemingly abandoned institute, the man finds an opening barely two feet above the ground. Inside he sees a ladder. He climbs the ladder and finds himself in front of a closed door. Opening the door, the man finds a room.

5

THE MAN CLOSES THE DOOR
TO THE ROOM BEHIND HIM.
A SPECTRAL GLOW DEFINES
SPACE AND THE HAZE IS
WELCOMED LIKE A TIRED
NIGHT. IN THE CENTER
OF THE ROOM THERE IS
A CIRCULAR MIRROR,
BARELY LARGER THAN
THE TILE OF A BATHROOM
FLOOR. THE MAN REMOVES
HIS CLOTHES BEFORE
FACING THE MIRROR.

—The dark smells holy, he says.

*Positioned on his knees, fore-arms flat upon the ground, his ass raised in the air.*

—Look, all bodies resemble the religious act of suppuration. Christ's wound exists only to be penetrated. Bodies are all made in God's image.

*His hole gapes.*

—If I could crawl inside myself and discover viscera from a personal perspective then I, too, could resurrect out of auto-annihilative (re-)birth.

*The limbs of the man spread out as if to reorient their posture into an explorable position.*

—There is a direct line between the thought of my sex and the wound my body offers to the world.

*For male sexual desire exists by way of absence as much as the postulation of woman's physical sexuality.*

—I can feel a rod through my body as if psi-phenomena were not contingent upon extra-sensation, but instead intra-sensation. The gasp of breath following exertion, the dizzying heights presented in the face of vertigo. The body's heights can only be reached in an attempt to eclipse limits: any exploratory interior life desires nothing more than excess.

*His index finger rims the rough skin surrounding the hallway of the dark sex. If the body is a temple then a man's anal cavity is the corridor that accesses the inner chamber.*

—My life can only be considered in relation to desire.

*Desire placed in resemblance to physical sensation can only be the chill of a sea gale, not the warmth of burial.*

—To re-encounter desire is to reconsider the self, to know
the self.

*The man feels a chill as his fingers begin to gently prod his hole.*

—I can only hope to die in a monsoon, or a tornado,
or to encounter my last thought as my body is thrust
against rocks in the sea, flesh tearing from flesh until an
unaccountable absence takes over all ontological sense
of embodiment. If I cannot think, I am, therefore, not.

*The front sex of man, imagined by many as a resonant
verticality in worship to god or the sun is instead a stake to
hold a body closer to the earth.*

—My mind can only serve as reminder to my body of
the sensate gestures it enacts, corporeal figurations of
limitless desire. An excess.

*Silence.*

*A cry of penetration.*

—O eye of night.

—I believe in you.

—I believe in the thought of the hole.

—I believe in you.

—O frozen void.

—I believe in you.

—O night of this eye, this hole, this wound.


*The light dissolves upon the man, body pooled in sweat, a time
for rest.*

6

Having crossed to the other side of the world the man inhabits the absence that guides his perpetual movement. His body pulsates desire but there is no body present, not even his own. He becomes like a thought and refuses to leave the space of existence. Contrary to expectation, he has crossed beyond finitude and finds himself neither live nor dead. His absent meditations pass a threshold defined only by what can be ontologically unknowable, which is to say there's an impossibility to what it could be said he becomes.

The night, the depth of the sea, the very darkest & most inaccessible entrance to the man's cavernous ass.

In this darkness he encounters only

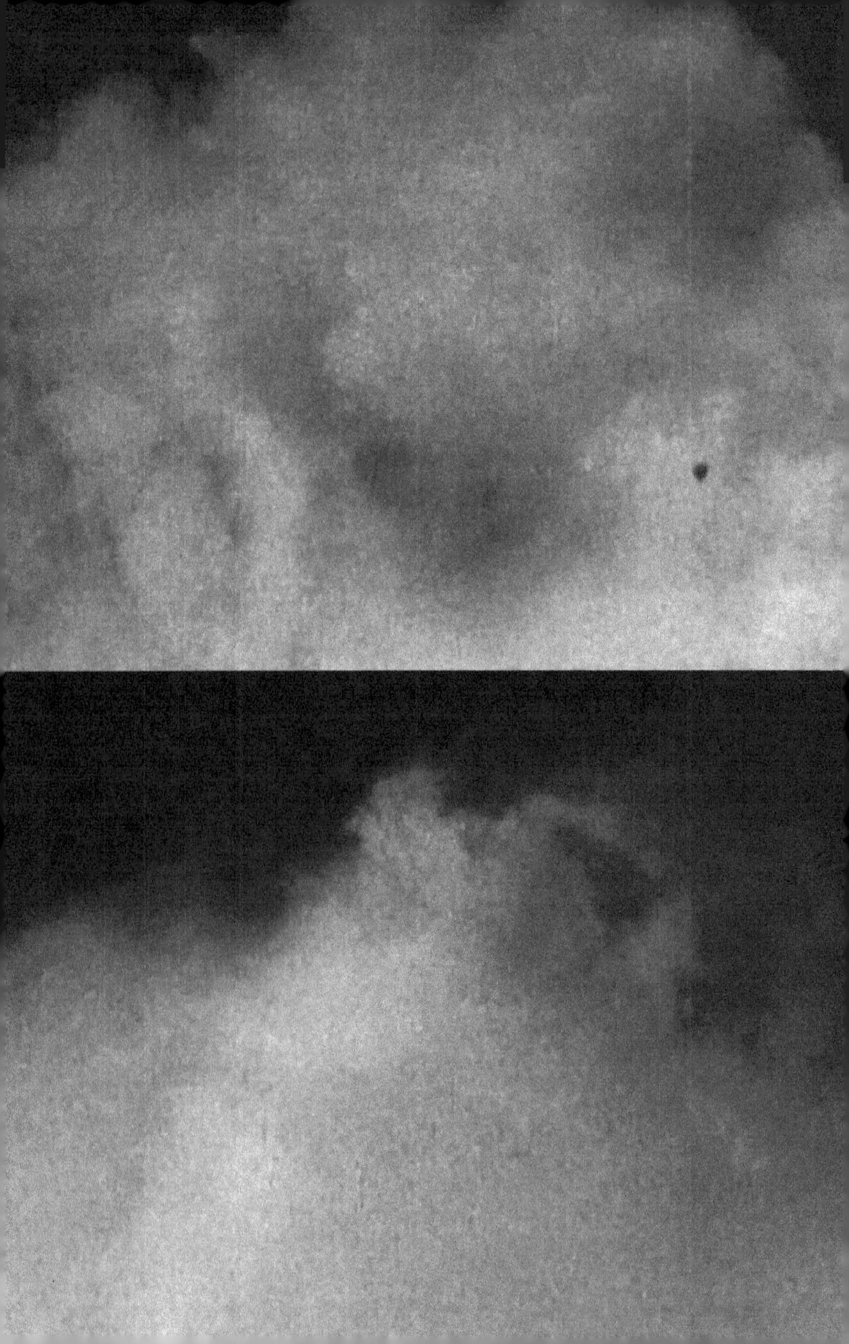

# [SOMETHING LIKE SEEING IN THE DARK]

# 7

*The figure calculates the movement of the body*
*The figure corrects errors the shake determines*
*The figure consults the screen for recommendation*

*re-articulate the calculation*
*is the first solution*

*establish the necessary trajectory*
*for the first mistake*
*the second and the third*

$\downarrow$

*the body of the man stands forward*
*to encounter a new figure before him*
*the unique principle*
*of unmotivated desire*

*there will be a struggle*
*and a total of five violations*
*will result in punishment*
*to the sound of nine voices*

*the violations were: the black mark, the aphonic*
*vocalization, amputation of the extremities, insensate*
*penetration, the final not mentioned*

↓

*the crimes committed without awareness can be
regarded as crimes committed by the night; as such the
severity of punishment can be tempered*

↓

*the nine voices were:*

*the sound of waves crashing
the sound of volcanic eruption
the sound of the earth's creak
the sound of flesh being slopped
the sound of beast being slaughtered
the sound of a dog's bark
the sound of terror
the sound of dirt trod by heavy boots
the sound of the cut, the lash*

*a single voice could never expect
to compete with the whole*

↓

*errors committed in waking life are liable only
to those who insist upon temporal linearity
timeless space insists upon a night
a physical retribution*

*↓*

*to the sound of waves crashing the man's memory was probed, reconfigured into a space of echo and physicality. to the sound of volcanic eruption the man's legs were bruised by rock. to the sound of the earth's creak the man's body was covered with the yolk of murre eggs.*

*to the sound of flesh being slopped, to the sound of beast being slaughtered, to the sound of a dog's bark, the man's final punishment was executed. the remaining sounds were voiced only in internment between the sounds guiding the punishments.*

*it was expected that the absent man would scream, but he did not.*

*↓*

*When a man dies his body is assumed to be complete. Within this finitude the body is often buried beneath the earth, burned to ashes, or thrown into the sea.*

*Thus the man, after recovering from this death, was shocked to find his physicality present. The stick of the yolk cocooned him glittery chrysalis; his legs would be sore for days. His death could be none so much as a nearing closer to something beyond. He knew that the result of his final punishment was yet to be understood.*

8

The figure of another is before him. Dead, in a corporeal way. A mode of death distanced from his own. An unrecoverable stasis. The video screens in the room that surrounds him all tuned to static.

The man is stretched out on a metal operating table. He is strapped in place. The physical death before him is hung from ceiling rods, floated above, before him. He notices a drip of intestinal leakage covers his own sex. The appendage rises to reach the dead body above him but when confronting a primal scene, such as this, there can be only an eternally recurring dissatisfaction. The man shuts his eyes and imagines the voice of a woman floating through the hallway out the door.

The being of another is impossible in this moment.

He knows that, somehow, he must leave.

9

*The woman is speaking to him in a calm tone. a vocalization so muted
and consistent he assumes the voice is coming from a cassette tape. But
he sees the woman before him. The woman exists in a proximity to his
physicality. He recognizes—with a sense of urgency—the woman as
someone important. A friend he has not seen in years, perhaps, or a lover
he could not fully give himself over to. The woman speaks a name to
him, a name unrecognizable as his own. The voice resounds in the cold
chamber: all of the rooms of the institute resemble a tomb.*

*He knows his eyes are either shut or open but, no matter what neurological
impulses are fired to his cortex, what is before him, the woman, seems
to flicker: he is blinking too fast, a light in the room strobes, the visual
acuity of the physical world falters.*

*He realizes the woman is speaking as if to hypnotize him, as if to allow
him to recall the absence he has just encountered. The man's body is
violently opposed to this, for he knows that when one crosses the border
into the realm of the impossible the experience shall not be forgotten, but
rather never encountered. The voice is so calm, so reassuring, so defiant
of what it is that his body wants to scream. A simultaneous desire to
both resist and accept. The waves outside, they're so calm, they're so
insistent, they're so eternal.*

>>>>>>>>>>>>>>>>>>>>>>>>>>>>>>>>>>>>>>>>>

> I'd like you to imagine that you are walking through a
> beautiful garden teeming with all kinds of wildflowers,
> hundreds of lilac bushes, and flowering trees. Perhaps
> you remember the garden you walked through to reach
> the institute from the boat. This is the garden you are
> in now. The trees are in full bloom. It is a warm, sunny
> day and a gentle breeze carries the sweet scent of the
> lilacs throughout the garden.

As you walk along you are happy. You are carefree and very relaxed. The sweet fragrance of the lilacs fills your senses. Walking along and taking in the colors and scents of the garden, you come upon three, small, one-room houses, all in a row. They all have signs in their front yards. The one on the left says "Motive of Your Past Lives." The one in the middle says "Motive of Your Present Life" and the one on the right says "Motive of Your Future Lives."

*To frame the question architecturally provides the man with a context he is comfortable holding on to. He is comfortable with the three, small, one-room houses. When a house is reduced to a room it becomes understandable. In many rooms murders are decided.*

You choose to enter the house on the left.

You reach for the door knob and enter.

You close the door behind you and find yourself standing in a pure white space in which the walls, ceiling and floor are entirely covered with chrome shower heads, all pointing towards the center of the room. You know this is not an ordinary shower. You know that this is a mysterious light shower. You feel safe and secure here. You know you can relax and fully enjoy the experience without worrying.

You walk to the center of the room and say "ON."

You are immediately engulfed in a continuous stream of brilliant, bluish-white light particles coming from all directions. The particles remind you of the sea.

The light stream feels like water bouncing off your body but you don't get wet. You know that, despite the unceasing water, you can never drown. The light stream feels very soft, warm, and soothing as it bounces against your body. It feels so good and you feel so happy you want it to last forever. However, the light shower will automatically turn off in 20 seconds.

*The warmth of the shower is something the man's body has refused for years. It's a position his own death, and his recovery from this death, has always refused. To allow comfort, the man would always insist, was to allow weakness. To allow weakness was to open yourself to the possibility of fear. To allow fear was to refuse the route toward the impossible.*

When the shower stops you will be in your primary past life. Twenty... nineteen... eighteen... feeling so relaxed... seventeen... sixteen... fifteen...

going deeper and deeper... fourteen... relaxing more and more with each breath...

thirteen... twelve... eleven... feeling more and more relaxed with each number...

ten... nine... eight... listening only to my voice...

seven... six... five... you are almost there...

four... three... two... and...

one...

You are now in your primary past life and are excited to experience what is ahead... Take a few moments to experience the sensations... the sounds... the smells... and the sights around you... nod if you can hear me...

*The man nods.*

↓
↓
↓
↓
↓

*The man wakes up to the rough sounds of ocean waves. He feels fully rested, and finds the soft wood his body is postured against comfortable in a way he never would have expected. While he knows that he should not make himself seen, he is not worried about the repercussions of having stowed away on the cargo ship. He is going to meet his oldest friend, a woman he feels a great kinship with, whom he has not seen in years. Looking out of a porthole he can see the island, home to a great research institute, in the distance. As the boat draws nearer he readies himself for the experience that awaits.*

[BY MEANS
OF WHICH
CLOSURE
& RAPTURE
COINCIDE, ALL
CIRCULARITY
MUST BE
DISRUPTED;
REFUSED]

No, you did not die. You did not fall over the side of the ship, your body crashing below to the sea. You did not scream. You did not shout to those aboard: do something fast. You did not feel your body pulled into the current below, your leg did not get caught in the motor. You did not pass out from loss of blood during your ride in the rescue helicopter. You did not arrive at the hospital unconscious. You did not become delirious in that anesthetized hospital room. You were not rolled through the hallways among cadavers on a cart. You did not stay in the emergency room for the entirety of that long night. You did not find me at a loss for words when asked by a doctor if I had contact information for your nearest relatives. You were not always alone in this world. You did not slip into a coma after a surgical procedure failed to have any positive effect. You did not know that I stopped coming to the hospital after a few days because every day the doctors told me they did not expect you to last. You never had your still hand in my own. You did not sleep like the dead. You did not die a prolonged & violent death at the hands of machinery penetrating the sea. You were not laid out in the morgue. You were not where I was looking for you.

No, I did not die. I did not fall over the side of the ship, my body crashing to the sea below. I did not scream. I did not shout at those aboard: do something fast. I did not feel my body pulled into the current below, my leg did not get caught in the motor. I did not pass out from loss of blood during my ride in the rescue helicopter. I did not arrive at the hospital unconscious. I did not become delirious in that anesthetized hospital room. I was not rolled through the hallways among cadavers on a cart. I did not stay in the emergency room for the entirety of that long night. I did not find you at a loss for words when asked if you had contact information for my nearest relatives. I was not always alone in this world. I did not slip into a coma after a surgical procedure failed to have any positive effect. I did not know that you stopped coming to the hospital after a few days because every day the doctors told you that they did not expect me to last. I never had my still hand in yours. I did not sleep like the dead. I did not die a prolonged & violent death due to the hands of machinery penetrating the sea. I was not laid out in the morgue. I was not where you were looking for me.

[ THE SEA IS NEVER STILL
THE ISLAND IS NEVER
EMPTY

THE NIGHT IS NEVER
QUIET                                    ]

LIMITLESSNESS

"I EQUATE LOVE (BODIES TOUCHING INDECENTLY)
WITH THE LIMITLESSNESS OF BEING—WITH NAUSEA,
THE SUN, AND DEATH."

*La scissiparité*
(Georges Bataille, 1949)

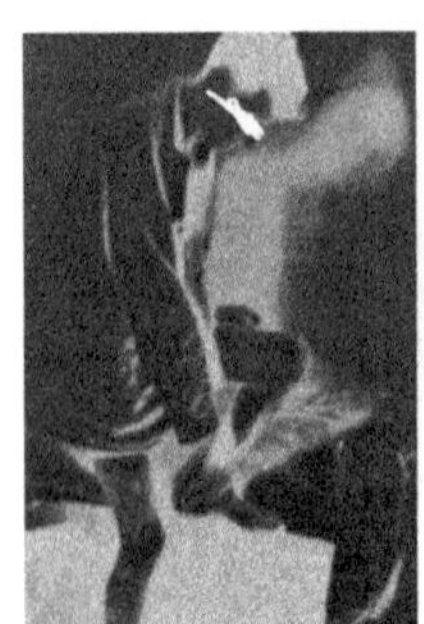

the genesis begins in the dark
as if the call of night
invites the weakness

the sound of the storm or
the line of light
penetrating, wounding
the shadow of sky

if there is nothing to touch
the thought can be passed

from one

to another

inside of a secret
& next to that of the other

there is nothing to position

207

A LINE

WHAT PLACE LOSES ME

WHAT POINT FINDS ME AGAIN

WHAT CRY MAKES ABYSS IN THE VOICE

TO CALL & CALL & REST

DISPENSING THE VOICE TO THE WORD

THE LUMP OF EARTH

the conjecture of body & float
as if placation could reveal the connection
of one body with
another

as if the extension of communication
could dominate the call for assistance

or the reverie of desire

& the word
dying of uncertainty
next to that of another
the body

the insistence upon
any remembrance
or the insistence upon
any narrative

the world permits
what the word does not

& within this space
what can be found is an absence

wounded skin
suppuration
the drip

effluvia as connectivity
or the response

one to
another

the debased body
toward the night

in contrast to existence

a portal
the revelation of

        the other side of

but inside this
acknowledged penetration
knowledge becomes detached
from experience
and the habitation
echoes the unknowable enigma
of an absent abyss

in counting
rhythmic hold

resistance
the push forward

TO NOT ASK OF
THE BODY

TO NOT ASK
THE BODY

forgetting the distance
from the cave to the sea

processional

the held casket heavy
the weight echoing gravity
in its push toward the ground

(the base horizon of
 the dead)

the sun pushes beyond

expectorating orifices
spectral spill

flesh

to another one can only
become

to the self one can only
flee

IN THE SUN
MY BODY POSITIONED
TOWARD LIGHT

IN THE SUN
THE TOUCH OF MY BODY
TO THE STONE

IN THE SUN
THE NIGHT FLEES MEMORY
& THE DAY ENCASES
THOUGHT

at the threshold of the void
the voice delivers a simple story
in a complex manner

to bury the sex
and live in glass

the thought follows
of disappearance from the village
replacement in earth

REJECTION
REJECTION
REJECTION
REJECTION
REJECTION
REJECTION

(& all this culpable desire)

the existence performed
outside of the other
outside of the body
instead
the ground
the earth
the dirt


SHAKE

NOTEBOOK

Silence.
Dramatization.
Explosion.
Transparency.
Here are some words: they mark the gradations of the experience; they are essentials, and yet they say nothing. Whoever writes them immediately encounters the inexpressible. Another language would be necessary. One despairs of writing, yet even so one chooses to write. The writing too begins from the other side of despair. How can this way be told now? Every discursive account is a betrayal. Writing must be the experience of the experience. It is not concerned with relating but with awakening. Then, language being what it is, there is only to trap it, pervert it, hole it in order to seize there the flash that no word can say, but that a certain configuration of words can seal. The rhythm will speak; the image will become the new language's word.

—"Poetry and Experience",  Bernard Noël

•

literalize the idea of hunting the void

•

corps/text » "cortext" » body/text

•

in absence, eroticism lingers

•

maze as execution chamber

•

the desire to encounter one's own corpse

•

*of violence & elevation*

•

*the paradoxical attempt to represent an ineffable aspect
of existence*

•

*the subject who speaks has just vanished*

•

ritualistic re-enactment of plot events

•

fiction as speculative encounters with the impossible

•

For instance, verticality can refer to the axis of transcendence, where transcendence refers to objectification, conceptualization, distanciation, homogeneity, knowledge, history (as written or as narrative) and, more generally, to the domain of theory, especially in the sense of theoria: to see. Horizontality, on the other hand, refers to immanence, and thus, secondarily, to ritual, difference, horror, silence, heterogeneity, abjection... and more generally, to the domain of the non-discursive, or practice...

> —*The Gift of the Open Hand: Le Corbusier Reading Georges Bataille's "La Part Maudite"* by Nadir Lahiji

•

> *the power of the sacred lies in its ambiguity and violence*

•

> make the text become a place of ruination and madness

•

...what Bataille calls an 'inner experience' is neither interior nor an experience but rather communication with the Outside.

> —*Dark Gaze* by Kevin Hart

•

are the ghosts producing words or are the words producing ghosts

•

...the more we take flight upward, the more our words are confined to the ideas we are capable of forming; so that now as we plunge into that darkness which is beyond intellect, we shall find ourselves not simply running short of words but actually speechless and unknowing.

—Pseudo-Dionysius, "The Mystical Theology"

•

The point here is that in the destruction of the self and the structure that gives it its meaning, a new language is born. Or rather, this new language remains forever in the process of being created within the previous structure. The new grammar is one of disequilibrium and ambiguity, thus retaining the capability for regeneration (and thus creativity). Virtual death begins to give birth to new meaning, new space, and new time.

—Aldith Gauci, *The Exhausted Body in Performance*

•

*to become an image is also to make an image,*
*a dynamic process that is also an act of physical agency*

•

*écriture a jourée de vide*

•

What do we seek, since the first traces of hands impressed in rock
the long, hallucinated perambulation of men across time, what do
we try to reach so feverishly, with such obstinacy and suffering,
through representation, through images, if not to open the body's
night, its opaque mass, the flesh with which we thick—and present
it to the light, or our faces, the enigma of our lives.

> —Philippe Grandrieux,
> "Sur l'horizon insensé du cinéma"

•

Call it mystical, supernatural, spiritual, whatever you like.
Whatever helps. I prefer to call it the future.

> —John Duncan

•

the flow of the cosmos merges allegorically in order
to be released in bodily desecration

•

It is said that God screams alone in space (or whatever we should call the dark celestial emptiness that encloses us all), screams alone at night and creates the vibration which has set everything in motion since the beginning of time, set off the brief pulsations and cycles we know as the sanctity of everyday life and the joy of life on Earth.

—Leif Elggren

•

It is time to abandon the world of the civilized and its light. It is too late to want to be reasonable and learned, which has led to a life without attractions. Secretly or not, it is necessary to become other, or else cease to be.

—Georges Bataille, "The Sacred Conspiracy"

•

Seek the extremes, that's where all the action is.

—Lee Lozano

•

atheological verticalism

•

When I use the word violence, I don't intend to refer explicitly to content, to representation (though it can be said that there are occasionally images of violence throughout the texts collected here); rather, what's intended is the violence of language itself, a sort of severing, the way that words mark a page in resemblance of a knife marking skin. Language can easily violate in terms of speech: accusations, insults, etc. But this is boring, language limited to speech escapes the idea of language as raw physical material, as text.

Often it is this textual violence that gives way toward the impossible, that slightly-out-of-reach concept that haunts my work, my habits, perhaps even my existence. [...]

—M Kitchell, "The Wound in the Sun: Introduction"

•

private spectacle, the idea of the ungraspable

•

*a primitive, chthonic form of the sacred through a rapturous escape from the self*

•

how to become imperceptible

•

...if the body attains silence by violence or pleasure, what happens when it rediscovers speech?

—Bernard Noël

•

Nothing is more physical than the practice of mysticism.

—Lea Vergine

•

*The white space provides the sacrificial.* The space creates the sacred.

•

bordellos & haunted hauses / the obscene factory / metempsychotic evolution / the sex act as inexchangable phantasm / excavate voids / the chant & the echo

•

To dramatise: to show again the mental image to its sensory contents. In sum, to realise.

—Bernard Noël

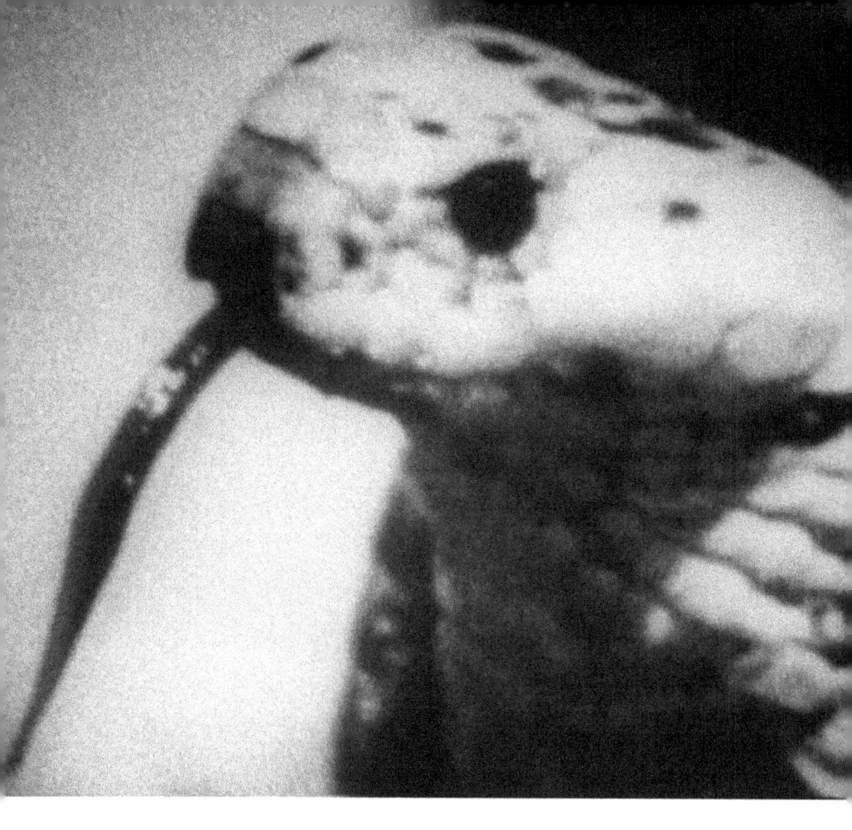

TO TRANSLATE THIS FASCINATION—THE BODY
& THE *BEYOND-THE-BODY*—INTO SOMETHING
ELSE... A FREEDOM IS NEEDED, OR PERHAPS
JUST A MORE THOROUGH EXPLORATION OF THE
CONSTRAINTS.

# VERTICALITY

- OBJECTIFICATION
- CONCEPTUALIZATION
- REPRESENTATION
- HOMOGENEITY
- KNOWLEDGE
- 'THEORY'

...

- THE ASCENSION OF ENERGY

# HORIZONTALITY

- IMMANENCE
- RITUAL
- DIFFERENCE
- HORROR
- SILENCE
- HETEROGENEITY
- ABJECTION
- 'PRACTICE'

AFTER ⚡ BEFORE

*The texts collected in this volume were written out of an exploratory desire to cross beyond the realm of "narrative of void-hunt" and into something new. They attempt to both dramatize the impossible and touch upon the sovereignty found in poetic effusion simultaneously; often by alternating back and forth between genres. They deliver a realm of work that directly preceded my desire, as as writer, to fully transcend the page and move towards a corporeal impossibility.*

*That is to say, there came a point where I no longer just wanted to write about levitating, I wanted my physical body to levitate.*

*Despite this work being inherently interstitial, there is value in what Allen S. Weiss refers to as excavating voids: "Investigate the hollow spaces of the text, the gaps between the lines, the silences between the words. Seek not exquisite corpses but disquieting cuts."*

*And now? Now I can no longer call myself a writer.*

*I cannot yet articulate what it is I'm on the path to becoming. The idea of my "identity" (or perhaps "role") is less interesting than my desire for impossible experience; this is the throughline of all of my work. While in my process, the text has not been fully abandoned, I have replaced my interest in the shape of the book with an interest in experimenting with the shape of a body.*

*Hindsight reveals that it was these textual labyrinths that lead the way. None of my work has ever been anything but inherently experimental; not in terms of classification, but in terms of what it is that I'm trying to do. Experimenting with narrative, experimenting with photography, experimenting with layout. Experimenting with a (my) body. The text has never been an end-point, it has always just been process, experience.*

*meta-morphosis*
by Michel Camus


becoming non-becoming
swelling by gradually losing our husk
swelling from the outside towards the inner-interior
swelling from the skin of the soul towards the center of the "body"
                              towards the fire at the center
                              towards the lightning
swelling, burning us under the sun of the dead
              to obliterate us for "the Unknown"
                          (conciousness without us)
returns to the center of itself the seed of eternity
the eye of death in direct sunlight.

becoming non-becoming: impossible?
the Impossible of life is the infinite possibility of death


                                        1978
                                        (translated by M Kitchell)

PRELUDE TO TRANSGRESSION

M KITCHELL

ISBN-13: 978-1-7352901-2-6



EDITED BY JOHN TREFRY,
DESIGNED & TYPESET BY M KITCHELL
TYPESET USING EHRHARDT MT & BOOGIE LT STD

THIS IS A TEXT OCCUPYING THE EXPANDED FIELD OF LITERATURE,
FROM INSIDE THE CASTLE
HTTP://INSIDETHECASTLE.ORG

"IN THE SILENCE / ALL EXTREMES ARE ALIKE."
—ROBERTO JUARROZ

www.ingramcontent.com/pod-product-compliance
Lightning Source LLC
Chambersburg PA
CBHW061119100726
47911CB00013B/611